KARTUSCH

written by: Stephen Cosgrove
illustrated by: Robin James

A Serendipity Book

Dedicated to Hazel Stevens and Rose Blanchard. Two people who opened my heart so that I could see.

Stephen
Cosgrove

A time or two ago, in a country corner of the forest, lived a dozen or so small creatures called Furry Eyefulls.

The Eyefulls were chubby little animals covered from head to toe with long fuzzy fur and two of the largest eyes you have ever seen.

All day long they would walk along the many trails of the forest, with their wide eyes open, looking for beautiful things to see. Sometimes they would stop for hours and hours just to gaze at a mountain bathed in morning sunshine.

They were known to sit on the beach and stare at their mirrored reflections in the lake.

Once in a while, a glistening fish would flash to the surface making ripples on the water. The Furries would roll about in fits of laughter, as their faces danced about the lake.

In the evening time, as all was getting dark, they would carefully gather twigs and sticks with which to make a fire. As the blackness of night settled about them, they would gaze forever at the stars in the sky or simply watch the dying embers of the fire.

Beauty was all around them and they never missed seeing anything.

But, even with the Furry Eyefulls there were problems. For, you see, the Furries were so afraid of not seeing something that was beautiful, that they never closed their eyes and never went to sleep. Now, all this just caused the Furry Eyefulls to become grumbly and grouchy. You know as well as I do that if you don't get some sleep you can get awfully cranky and sometimes downright mean.

At least once a day one of the Furries, who wasn't looking where he was going, would bump into another Furry and, before you could say Furry Eyefull four times, there would be a fluffy pile of Furries all grumbling and mumbling at each other and nobody saying I'm sorry.

Well, things could have gone on like this forever, had it not been for one small Furry who stopped to watch a bright green snake who was wrapped around the stem of a flower. All the other Furry Eyefulls crowded around the stem to see what he was looking at. They bustled and shoved and grumbled and growled at each other as the beautiful little snake wound softly to the top of the flower.

"Who's there?" he asked quietly as his tongue flicked gently about and tasted the air.

"Would you look at that!" said one of the Furries. "That snake is blind, for he has no eyes with which to see."

Words of pity rang out from the Furry Eyefulls: "He's blind!" "He can't see!" and "Oh you poor, poor snake!"

"Well!" said the snake, "my name is Kartusch, and I would hardly call myself poor."

"But you must be poor!" one of them said, "For you cannot see all the riches of the beautiful forest."

"Ah," said Kartusch, "beauty is not just in seeing things. It's also in touching and feeling and hearing things." And with that Kartusch listened very quietly and heard the beautiful forest growing in the warm spring air.

Well, the Furry Eyefulls were not to be out-done by a green snake. So they began listening very hard to hear this beauty but once again somebody slipped or, maybe he was pushed, and the grumbling and mumbling started all over again.

Kartusch listened around and then laughingly said, "You call me poor for I cannot see, yet you must be poorer for you cannot hear."

"Oh, yes we can!" they said. "Just listen to this!" And with that they tried with all their might to listen to the beauty around them. But . . . somebody coughed, somebody sneezed, and then somebody banged somebody on the knees. And then everybody started grumbling and mumbling again.

"It's no use!" said one of the Furries. "We'll never be able to listen. None of us ever gets any sleep because we're afraid we might miss something beautiful. And because we don't get any sleep we'll always be grumbly; and because we're grumbly we'll never get to hear anything beautiful."

Kartusch smiled a secret smile and slid down the flower to the grass below and wound himself up on a tall mushroom.

"Gather around," he whispered, "and I shall teach you how to listen!"

All the Furry Eyefulls crowded about trying to get close to the emerald snake.

"Now all of you," said Kartusch, "sit very quietly and softly close your eyes."

The Furries sat down with a bump on the grass and after squirming around for a bit they all, one by one, began to close their eyes and listen.

"I can hear it!" exclaimed one. "I can hear something beautiful." And sure enough off in the distance each one of them began to hear the soft, quiet beauty of an evening cricket.

"Keep listening," said Kartusch, "and you not only will feel the wondrous things around you but in your mind you will dream of all the beauty you have seen today."

One by one the Furries gently fell asleep as the sounds of evening wove their dream-like spell.

Kartusch listened to the soft sounds of night around him and he thought, "I may not be able to see with my eyes but I can see all that I need to see when I listen with my mind." And with that he fell fast asleep.

YOU MAY SEE ALL THAT IS
    AROUND YOU
BUT YOU MAY FEEL NOTHING AT ALL.
SO TRY AND CLOSE YOUR EYES
    SO TIGHT
AND LISTEN TO THE NIGHT TIME FALL.